A
Nightingale
CHRISTMAS
A NOVEL

A Nightingale CHRISTMAS

A NOVEL

HEATHER HOLM

SWEETWATER BOOKS
AN IMPRINT OF CEDAR FORT, INC.
SPRINGVILLE, UTAH

© 2011 Heather Holm
All rights reserved.

This is a work of fiction. The characters, names, incidents, places, and dialogue are products of the author's imagination, and are not to be construed as real.

ISBN 13: 978-1-59955-912-4

Published by Sweetwater Books, an imprint of Cedar Fort, Inc.
2373 W. 700 S., Springville, UT 84663
Distributed by Cedar Fort, Inc., www.cedarfort.com

LIBRARY OF CONGRESS CATALOGING-IN-PUBLICATION DATA

Holm, Heather, 1956- author.
  A nightingale Christmas / Heather Holm.
     pages cm
  Summary: A woman is disfigured in an airplane crash, and after witnessing a
series of miracles, she is able to cope with her deformities and accept a new way
of life.
  ISBN 978-1-59955-912-4
  1. Christmas stories. 2. Domestic fiction. 3. Christian fiction. 4. Aircraft
accidents--Fiction. 5. Disfigured persons--Fiction. 6. Wounds and injuries--
Psychology--Fiction. 7. Body image--Fiction. I. Title.
  PS3608.O494324N54 2011
  813'.6--dc22

                                   2011010919

Cover design by Angela D. Olsen
Cover design © 2011 by Lyle Mortimer
Edited and typeset by Heidi Doxey

Printed in the United States of America

10 9 8 7 6 5 4 3 2 1

Printed on acid-free paper

Inspired by and dedicated to
the victims of the
January 13, 1982,
Air Florida Flight 90 tragedy
and
in gratitude to the
courageous souls who
risked their lives to save
five of those victims.

MESSIAS

From the depths of my soul you came
Hailing the misty morning dawn
And cursing the darkened shadows
of mine anguished mind.

Amid the endless fears and broken dreams you stood
To chastise hidden demons of despair,
To save this fallen, aching soul,
And close the awesome gates of hell.

ONE

The familiar strains of Christmas carols drifted through the building, and squeals of delight signaled Santa's arrival in the children's ward down the hall. Christmas was three days away, but I didn't care. The holidays were a reminder of what I had lost and what I would never have again.

For the hundredth time that day, my eye traced the outlines of the cinder blocks in the walls of my hospital room. In the many times I had counted them, I could never get past 150. How pitiful! It seemed I had nothing better to do with my time.

During the past twelve months, I had come to think of these white disinfected halls as the only home I had ever known. From the moment I regained consciousness until the time I was finally able to exist without feeling horrible pain, I had struggled to remember, to put the pieces of my life back together so I might live it again. But it was no use. I had no idea who I was.

The doctors told me I was a victim of a plane crash—a passenger in a Boeing 737 that, due to a port engine fire, clipped a power generator and plowed into the icy waters of a nearby river. As was reported in the local newspaper, only a few "fortunate" individuals survived, but I often wondered just how fortunate I really was.

I came from nowhere—all bodies and survivors had been identified. No other names were listed by the airline as having boarded that ill-fated plane, and none of the other surviving passengers could identify me. Every possible effort was made to discover my identity, but in the end, my age, which was estimated at twenty-four, was the only thing they could tell me about my past.

After being stabilized, I was rushed by helicopter to the nearest burn center. My only memories of that time were ones of tremendous pain. A series of skin grafts, pressure suits, facial masks, and physical and mental therapy were the norm. Unfortunately, nothing short of plastic surgery, which I could not afford, would take away the horrendous scars.

One by one, my fellow survivors were allowed to return home to their families. I didn't know if I had a home, let alone a family. Who was I, and what was I to do with my life? Wouldn't it have been better for me to die? Words could not describe the painful abyss that had become my life.

They called me Jane Doe, although having a name meant little to me since I no longer felt human. I was scarred beyond recognition and severely deformed. Three of the fingers on my left hand were missing, as were my hair and large portions of my ears and nose. I walked with a limp, and my left foot was partially burned away. I was blind in one eye, and the other eye needed a corrective lens.

All of my injuries were horrific, but what bothered me most were my damaged vocal cords. I hated the sound of my voice. I found it easy to avoid mirrors but nearly impossible to keep from talking.

Day after day I found myself in one of the treatment rooms with the other burn victims who were undergoing group therapy. But this day was different. It was almost Christmas, and we were to have visitors—volunteers composed mostly of local residents who wanted to help ease our pain.

Meg, our therapist, told us, "Now, I know this will not be easy. These people mean well and are sincere in their desire to help you. It can be a pleasant experience for everyone—if you let it be. As always, it will depend on your attitude."

I knew she was talking to me. My attitude hadn't been as good as it could be, but on the other hand, I didn't see any reason to change it. I wanted desperately to believe I had a family—a family who loved me and would be at my side if they knew my circumstances—but I wouldn't allow myself the luxury of believing this. The fire not only destroyed my body, but also my spirit. I felt nothing. I couldn't allow myself to feel anything.

A group of nurses led us to the visitors' lounge. What a sight we made, shuffling along, some of us having difficulty walking, and some of us so badly deformed we didn't look human. I felt sorry for myself, just as I had so many times before. I didn't care about Christmas, and I didn't care about the people who came to visit. I just wanted to go back to my room and hide.

I sat apart from everyone and turned my face to the wall. I didn't want anyone staring at me. It was bad enough that I was a freak without having it mirrored in people's faces.

Suddenly, I felt a light touch on my arm. I thought I was imagining it, but then I felt it again. I looked up into the face of a beautiful young woman. Her eyes were filled with compassion and a sadness that I could not comprehend. She showed no sign of shock or horror as she looked at me and said, "Hello. I saw you sitting by yourself. You looked so . . . lonely. I thought I'd come say hi."

After getting over the initial surprise of her greeting, I heard my horrible, cracked voice answer, "Yes, I guess I am lonely." Then I turned back to face the wall. She talked to me for over an hour. I don't remember what she said, but as she talked, I found myself enjoying the gentle sound of her voice and the sincere warmth of her company.

All too soon the day came to an end, and with its close came my visitor's departure, leaving me with an overwhelming sense of loss that I did not understand.

TWO

Someone was shaking me gently, and I woke to see a cherubic face hovering over me.

"G'mornin', sunshine!" the face said cheerfully. "Meg wants to see you in her office—ASAP."

I moaned. *Darn nurse!* I thought. *Why does she have to be so annoying?*

"Do you need help getting dressed?" she asked.

"No, April," I mumbled. "Gotta learn some-time."

"Don't go back to sleep, Jane," she persisted. "Meg has some good news." She bustled about the room, straightening anything that looked out of place and flinging open the curtains. "Don't you want to hear the good news?" she added excitedly.

It was no use. I had to get up. I never slept too well anyway, and when I did, I had terrible night-mares. I slowly dragged myself out of bed, and with the cherub's help got dressed and put on my wig.

We walked the short distance to Meg's office, where Meg greeted me warmly and asked me to make myself at home. We chatted briefly, and then Meg got down to business.

"Jane," she said, "have you thought about your future? You can't stay here forever. You need to get out into the world."

I sighed. I knew what was coming. My time to leave had arrived, and this was the moment I had been dreading. I felt hopeless and alone.

"It's almost Christmas—" I started to say, but she interrupted.

"It's natural for you to be frightened, but everything is going to be all right. We have something special planned for you."

Before finishing her sentence, Meg stood up and opened the door. She motioned to someone, and a young woman entered the room. I recognized her immediately as the woman who had been so kind to me the previous day.

"This is Lauren Jacoby. She has asked to have you stay with her in her home, at least for a while, until you get back on your feet. She's anxious to know your answer."

Becoming emotional but showing great restraint, the young woman told us that her sister had disappeared a year ago.

"We don't know if she is dead or alive. We don't know if she needs our help or if she is sick or being mistreated. I've lived in misery this past year not knowing where she is or what is happening to her. The authorities tell us the chances of her being alive are next to none. You see, I loved my sister," she added as she tried to maintain her composure. "Kellie had a lot going for her. She would never take her own life or do anything else to hurt herself. Even though we were miles apart, she kept in touch. We always knew where she was. Her disappearance nearly broke my parents' hearts."

The young woman paused. Then, still trying to control her emotions, she continued. "This past year I've immersed myself in visiting and caring for the sick and homeless, maybe for reasons that aren't entirely unselfish. If Kellie is out there somewhere, I pray that someone will show her the kindness I've tried to show others." Her voice broke, and she slowly reached out to me, gently touching my arm. "If I could only have part of her with me once more by helping you . . ."

The small office was suddenly quiet. Embarrassed, I squirmed uncomfortably in my chair.

"Well, what do you think?" Meg finally asked.

"I suppose it won't hurt to try," I answered in my raspy voice.

"So it's settled then," Meg announced. "Pack your things, and Lauren will take you to your new home. I'm happy for you," she added. "I think you'll come to love and enjoy Lauren and her family."

❧ ⬦ ⋯ ⬦ ❧

Meg slipped into my room as I was gathering my scanty belongings. She wanted to say good-bye.

"Jane," she said, "I know this is a godsend for you. Please don't worry. Everything is going to be all right." She paused briefly and then continued, "Lauren and her husband, Anthony, moved from California into this area about eight months ago when his employer transferred him. They have two small children—a boy and a girl. I think you'll enjoy being in their home. It will be like having a family of your own."

I looked down at my belongings on the bed. I didn't know what to say.

Meg gently took me in her arms and embraced me, and I found myself not wanting her to let me go. I was so frightened, lonely, and heartbroken. I hadn't cried at all since the accident. I honestly believed that tears would never flow again for me. At first I thought it was a blessing, but now I wasn't sure.

Together Meg and I walked to the nurses' station at the end of the hall where April and a wheelchair were waiting to transport me outside to Lauren's car. Lauren met us there, and as April pushed me toward the elevator, Lauren asked if she could do it instead. I briefly glanced back at Meg. She sincerely looked as though she would miss me, and I saw her wipe tears from her eyes as we entered the elevator and the doors closed behind us.

THREE

I was apprehensive about how Lauren's two children, ages four and six, would react to me. I figured her husband would be able to accept my appearance, but what about her children?

When we arrived at Lauren's home, both father and daughter seemed to welcome me with open arms, but it was different with the little boy. He was trying with all his might to conceal his terror. He finally started crying and ran for the nearest door. Lauren looked at me apologetically and followed him out. I had expected this, but it still hurt.

In contrast, the little girl seemed to take a genuine interest in me, as if she understood my misfortune and sincerely wanted to help. It was uncanny how much she resembled her mother.

Anthony, their father, uncomfortably began to apologize for his son's behavior, but his daughter interrupted. "Oh, don't mind my brother," she said. "He's a crybaby. He just doesn't like being around strangers, that's all. He'll be all right. He just has to get used to you." I couldn't help but notice her father smile slightly as he watched his daughter and listened to her comments.

After calming down her son, Lauren returned to the living room where we stood waiting.

"I'm sorry, Jane. I'm so sorry. He's just a child—only four years old. Please forgive him. He'll get used to you." She motioned for me to follow her. "Would you like to see your room?" she asked. "Lacie and I have been busy getting it ready. We're excited to see what you think."

"Oh yes," said the child bouncing up the stairs ahead of us. "I chose your bedspread and curtains. You're going to love them! They're cherry blossoms—just like Aunt Kellie used to love."

The room took my breath away. A lot of time and care had been taken to make it just perfect. Just as Lacie had said, the curtains and bedspread were covered with cherry blossoms. The morning sun shining through the window and into the room was one of the most beautiful sights I had ever seen. It was all too good to be true, but the real clincher came when Lauren opened the closet doors.

"Jane, I don't know how you'll feel about this, but you are Kellie's size," she said awkwardly. "I kept a few of her things. I was wondering if maybe you could put them to good use."

"Oh," I whispered almost reverently as I caught a glimpse of the wardrobe. I slowly approached the closet, and as I fingered each item of clothing, touched each pair of shoes, and smelled the soft, sweet fragrance of the closet, an unseen hand seemed to reach out to me, pulling me back in time. For a moment I thought I would remember, but it was not meant to be. As soon as the haunting feeling came over me, it quickly disappeared.

I stood in silence, looking past the clothing into the dark closet. Lauren waited patiently for me to speak.

"I can't wear these beautiful clothes," I finally said. "It would be a mockery to the memory of your sister."

Standing near Lauren, I could see and compare my scarred, deformed hands with her smooth, clear skin, and I realized for the first time how horrible I must appear to others. I let go of the rose-colored dress I was holding and dropped my arms to my sides.

Lauren seemed to sense my feelings. "I think you're being too hard on yourself," she said gently. "These clothes will fit you perfectly. I want you to have them. I think they're just what you need."

I looked up at her and saw she was sincere, and I marveled at her kindness.

FOUR

Gathering around the tree on Christmas Eve was a tradition in the Jacoby home. Anthony began the celebration by asking each of us what we were most thankful for. He said his greatest blessing was his wife and family, and Lauren agreed. Lacie was thankful for me being there, and Matthew was grateful for Christmas. They all looked at me expectantly, but I didn't know what to say.

"Why don't we sing Christmas carols while Jane thinks of something?" Anthony suggested.

Relieved, I mumbled a quiet thanks.

My mind reviewed the events of the past year, and I was certain I didn't have anything to be thankful for. Life was a nightmare, and I was powerless to do anything about it. My attitude changed, however, when Lauren's little family sang Christmas carols. Their sweet, sincere songs touched my heart, and I realized just how blessed I really was.

This dear family had accepted me with open arms and surrounded me with love and compassion. How many people in my circumstance are welcomed into a stranger's home to be sheltered, clothed, and fed? Their words calmed me, and for the first time since the accident, I felt tears coming to my eyes.

> Then pealed the bells more loud and deep:
> God is not dead, nor doth he sleep.

I once believed in God. I was sure of it! But if he did exist, why had he forsaken me?

When the family finished singing their carols, Anthony turned to me and asked, "Have you thought of what you're most thankful for, Jane?"

Without hesitation, I answered, "I'm most thankful for this family."

"Why, thank you, Jane!" Lauren said, pleased with the compliment.

"Yes, thank you," Anthony added, smiling.

After a short pause, he looked at Lauren and said, "Well, I guess it's time!"

Lauren reached down to the side of her chair and picked up a hand-carved wooden box. The children watched in anticipation as she opened it and gently removed a candle.

"We have a new tradition in our home," Lauren

explained. "Every year at midnight on Christmas Eve, we light a special candle in memory of my sister, Kellie, and all those who are suffering. After reading the Christmas story in Luke, we also offer a prayer in their behalf that God will carry them in his arms, bring them home safely, and make them whole."

Without further comment, Lauren lit the candle and placed it in a candleholder on the coffee table.

Anthony opened his Bible to the second chapter of Luke and read the story of the Savior's birth.

> And it came to pass in those days, that there went out a decree from Caesar Augustus, that all the world should be taxed . . .
>
> And all went to be taxed, every one into his own city.
>
> And Joseph also went up from Galilee, out of the city of Nazareth, into Judea, unto the city of David, which is called Bethlehem; . . .
>
> To be taxed with Mary his espoused wife, being great with child.
>
> And so it was, that, while they were there, the days were accomplished that she should be delivered.
>
> And she brought forth her firstborn son, and wrapped him in swaddling clothes, and laid him in a manger; because there was no room for them in the inn. (Luke 2:1-7)

Anthony closed his Bible and placed it on the end table. "It's time for our Christmas prayer," he announced. We all joined hands, and Anthony prayed.

I bowed my head, but I couldn't concentrate on his words. I kept thinking about God and wondering why he would allow such a terrible thing to happen to me. It suddenly got quiet, and I realized that the prayer was over. I looked up to see the children kissing their parents goodnight.

"I think it's time for two little yahoos to go to bed so Santa can come," Anthony remarked. "We'll be up later to tuck you in." Turning to me, he teased, "What about you, Jane? Do you want to be tucked in?"

"I want to be tucked in," Lauren said playfully as she put her arms around her husband. "I'll tuck Jane in if you'll tuck me in."

"You got it," Anthony said, and he kissed her.

"I'd like to stay down here by the Christmas tree for a few minutes, if you don't mind," I said.

"Sure," Lauren replied. "Let me know when you're ready to go to bed, and I'll come help you."

I waited until they had gone upstairs, and then I inched my way across the couch to the end table. I picked up the Bible and thumbed through the pages. It somehow slipped from my grasp and landed open-faced on the floor. As I painfully leaned over to retrieve it, my eye caught sight of some verses highlighted in yellow. I picked the book up and read:

> The Lord hath forsaken me, and my Lord hath forgotten me.
>
> Can a woman forget her sucking child, that she should not have compassion on the son of her womb? yea, they may forget, yet will I not forget thee.
>
> Behold, I have graven thee upon the palms of my hands. (Isaiah 49:14–16)

I was suddenly overwhelmed with emotion. I struggled to control my intense feelings, but it was no use. I wept uncontrollably. It was as if all the grief locked inside me was finally coming out. I looked up and saw Lauren coming toward me with open arms. In an instant, she was at my side, holding me and rocking me like a baby. Warm tears slipped from her eyes and landed softly on my face.

"I'm sorry!" I blubbered. "I'm so sorry! I don't know what came over me!"

"You don't need to apologize," Lauren said, gently lifting my face and looking into my eyes. "Would you like Anthony to say a prayer for you?"

"I think that's a good idea," Anthony said, his voice breaking with emotion. He had followed Lauren downstairs when they heard me crying.

I don't remember what Anthony said, but I clearly remember the peace I felt when he prayed for me that night. From that moment on, I knew that regardless of how difficult my future might be, everything was going to be all right.

FIVE

As the days passed, I felt increasingly comfortable with the Jacoby family. Spring came, and it was as if life had never been different. I enjoyed the children. Matthew was getting used to me and would sometimes sit on my lap in the evening after dinner. I grew close to Lacie, which was inevitable. Yet, still, I wanted to know who I was.

One evening, as we sat around the kitchen table eating dinner, Lacie, who had been high-strung all day, looked at me and exclaimed, "Please pass the rolls, Aunt Kellie, and the butter." An uncomfortable silence filled the room. Not realizing the impact of what she had just said, Lacie giggled.

Anthony quickly took her by the hand and led her into the living room. I wasn't sure what I saw on Lauren's face. Whether it was wonder and amazement or just plain grief, I could not tell. Then she quickly came to her senses.

"Don't mind Lacie," she said quietly. "She doesn't mean any harm. She and my sister were very close. For some reason, from the first day you walked into the house, Lacie made up her mind that you were Kellie. That's probably why she was so willing to accept you when Matthew was a little frightened at first. She so desperately wants you to be her Aunt Kellie that she's a little confused."

"I understand," I answered.

We could hear Lacie's high-pitched voice above the muffled tones of her father's as they spoke to each other.

"But she is!" Lacie cried. "Why don't you believe me, Daddy? See her eyes? They're Aunt Kellie's eyes! I'm not lying!"

"Lacie," Anthony replied, "I know you wouldn't lie, sweetheart, and I know you miss your Aunt Kellie, but you need to stop playing make-believe."

"But Daddy," she said, sobbing, "you don't understand!"

Lauren, with a faraway look in her eyes, softly and helplessly said, "If we only knew . . . If we only knew something for sure . . . anything . . . final."

It hurt to hear the truth. I'd started to believe that I actually did belong in this family. It wasn't just Lacie who was playing make-believe. I was also, and I needed to get hold of myself and face reality.

Later that evening I slowly and painfully groped my way down the darkened hall to Lacie's room. I knocked gently on the door.

"Go away," came the answer.

"Lacie," I whispered, trying to make my sandpaper voice sound as pleasant as possible. "Please let me in. I want to talk to you."

After a moment's pause, she slowly opened the door. Sullenly looking at the floor, she motioned for me to enter. She hopped under the covers, and I sat next to her on the bed.

"I know this sounds silly," I said haltingly, "but I have grown to love you, Lacie. If I had a little girl, I would want her to be just like you."

She kept her face toward the wall, but I could see the tears still damp on her cheeks.

"Aunt Kellie used to tell me that too," she replied. "You don't look like my Aunt Kellie, and you don't sound like her, but you are her. Daddy says I'm not supposed to make-believe anymore."

I uncomfortably readjusted my position on the bed. I was at a loss for words. "I wish I was," I finally answered. "You're not the only one who has been playing make-believe. I have been too."

She was quiet a few seconds, and then, almost defiantly, she announced, "I don't play make-believe."

Once again I found myself speechless. What could I say to this child to help her understand—to help her accept that her aunt was gone?

"Lacie," I tried again. "I'll tell you what. If you want me to be your aunt, I'll be your aunt. But we have to make rules. Call me Aunt Jane, okay? Don't call me Aunt Kellie, because it really hurts your mommy when you do."

She glanced at me with a knowing look as if to say, "Okay, I'll compromise if I must, but I know something you don't." She flipped her little face into the pillow and mumbled something inaudible.

I was touched by her grief. Kellie had been one lucky woman, and I wondered if she had known how lucky she was. Then I noticed the photo album partially hidden beneath Lacie's pillow.

"What's this?" I asked, pulling it out. As I did so, I got an immediate reaction.

"Don't!" she said, snatching it from me. "Mama doesn't know I have it!" She held it tightly to her little body as she would a favorite doll. She suddenly looked up at me in excitement and asked, "Hey! Do you want to see her?"

The invitation was unexpected, and a cold chill swept over me. I felt as if someone had walked on my grave—as if I had a grave to walk on. I immediately panicked. Part of me wanted to see Kellie and part of me didn't. Not waiting for my reply, Lacie opened the photo album to the first page. I soon found myself hesitantly sliding up next to her on the bed to see the pictures more clearly with my good eye.

"She's beautiful, isn't she?" Lacie commented, and I nodded my head, for Kellie was indeed beautiful. The face of the young woman smiling up at me from the photo was not as threatening as I thought it would be. Her countenance was kind, and her gentle features strongly resembled those of her sister.

As we continued to look through the album together, Lacie would pause every so often to tell me about a certain picture. She had a lot of beautiful memories, and I found myself deeply yearning for memories of my own.

"She truly was beautiful, Lacie," I said after we finished looking through the album. I turned out the light and tucked her in bed. She looked up at me through half-closed brown eyes, trying desperately to fight off sleep. "Please, Aunt Kellie," she said, half crying, half dreaming, "try to remember. I asked God in my prayers to help us find you, and he did. I've asked him to help you remember who you are, and I know he'll do that 'cause he always hears and answers my prayers."

I shook my head in the darkness. Oh, the faith of

a child! This would take much more than a simple prayer; this would take a miracle, and after what I'd been through, I no longer believed in miracles. My heart wept for Lacie, for Lauren, and for myself. The unfairness of it all! They'd lost a loved one, and I, in reality, had lost my life. I felt helpless and discouraged. I wanted to make things right, yet I knew I couldn't.

My natural feelings of affection had been stifled for some time, but as Lacie dropped off to sleep, I gently pushed the hair out of her face, caressed her blonde head, and softly kissed her on the cheek. I suddenly felt exhausted, and I lay down next to her on the bed and slept soundly until morning.

SIX

Summer mornings at the Jacoby home were my favorite time of day. Anthony would go to work, and after completing their chores, the children would go into the backyard to play. This left Lauren and me alone together. I loved our conversations. I was comfortable with her, and we could talk freely about almost anything.

On this particular morning, Lauren told me that her parents, Adele and Buzz Mitchell, were coming from California for a week-long visit and would arrive shortly after noon. I was somewhat apprehensive, but a feeling of excitement soon overcame my anxiety. I was curious about this couple. Their daughter thought they were perfect, and I felt as if I already knew them since they were the subject of so many of our conversations.

I stayed upstairs and watched their arrival from my bedroom window. They came in a taxi, and as

I watched, Lacie, Matthew, and Lauren ran out to meet them.

The Mitchells were an attractive elderly couple who appeared to be happy and content with their lives. Upon meeting them face-to-face, however, I noticed a sadness in their eyes that was probably caused by the loss of their daughter.

Lauren had mentioned to me earlier that her parents met and fell in love in their later years, and shortly thereafter two little girls joined them. Lauren came first, and Kellie arrived eighteen months later.

Lauren notified Anthony at his office, the children were called in from the backyard, and together we sat down as a family to eat our noon-day meal.

Lauren purposely seated me between her parents so we could get to know each other. "Mom, Dad," she announced. "This is Jane."

"How are you, Jane?" Mrs. Mitchell asked, taking my hands. She held them for at least a minute before squeezing them warmly and letting them go.

Neither of Lauren's parents drew back in fear or abhorrence at my appearance. Instead they both searched my face—in particular, my eyes. I saw nothing but goodness in their countenances, and for a moment, I thought I caught a glimmer of hope in their eyes as they met my gaze.

❧ ⬦ ⋯ ⬦ ❧

Lunch was a pleasant experience, and I enjoyed the Mitchells' company. I quickly learned that Lauren's parents were everything she said they were. Buzz Mitchell had a wonderful sense of humor and seemed to be everything I'd want in a father. Adele had the same qualities I admired in Lauren. She was gentle, kind, and compassionate—a true lady. I longed to be near them and get to know them better, but the week passed quickly, and it seemed that almost overnight it was time for them to return to California.

Buzz and Adele both hugged me before they left. Adele held me close for a long time. When she finally let me go, she said, "Jane, what are your plans for the future?"

Lauren blushed. "Mom," she said quietly. "Let's not talk about that now—"

"It's okay, Lauren," I assured her. "I know it's something I need to face." I awkwardly avoided Adele's gaze and said, "I'm technically a ward of the state—except that Lauren and Anthony have generously taken me in." Looking at Mrs. Mitchell, I continued, "I feel terrible about that, and I'm planning on carrying my own weight eventually. I hope to someday repay your daughter for her kindness—"

"Oh, don't worry about that!" Lauren interrupted. "We can take care of you as long as you need us to. My mother is just thinking about your happiness. No one can truly be happy without using their potential and making something worthwhile of their life. You have the right as a child of God to be happy. Everyone does. It's just that each of us is responsible for our own happiness."

Sensing my tender feelings, Mrs. Mitchell gently added, "I didn't mean to imply that you are a burden, Jane, because you aren't. We know that being self-sufficient isn't something you can do right now. Lauren and Anthony are perfectly happy to help you. I just wondered if you have any goals or dreams you'd like to pursue once you're feeling better. If possible, we'd like to help you achieve those goals."

"I guess I haven't thought that far ahead," I admitted, looking down at my scarred hands. "I'm not sure what to do. My face—everything—I look horrible . . ."

Adele tenderly lifted my face and looked into my eyes. "I can see how it would be hard for you to go into public," she said, "but you need to understand that true beauty comes from within. It's not what we look like on the outside that counts. It's what we are on the inside. You are beautiful, Jane, and you have so much to offer."

She kissed me on the forehead and reluctantly backed away. I nodded, but her words didn't make me feel any better. I couldn't find it in my heart to believe them.

That night, alone in my room, I reviewed the events of the day. I thought about how I had shut myself away from the rest of the world, never going outside the Jacoby home, seeing no one and speaking to no one. I was convinced that I must not deprive myself of a future just because I no longer had a past.

As I climbed into bed, I vowed that I would get a job and provide a living for myself. I would pick up the pieces of what was left of my life and earn the money to have my face reconstructed. I knew it would take every ounce of energy and courage I had to achieve this goal. It felt good to once more have a purpose in life, and I turned over on my side and fell into a peaceful sleep.

SEVEN

The next morning I discussed my plans with Lauren and asked for her support in my decision. She was more than happy to help, but at the same time, she seemed disappointed.

"I don't know, Jane," she said. "You're still weak. Do you think it would be a good idea for you to push it when you still aren't completely healed?"

"Well," I answered, "it's been over a year now since the accident, and I can't continue to be a burden on you and Anthony."

"Oh, Jane," she said, concerned, "have we ever made you feel that way? You've never been a burden. You've actually been a blessing to me."

"You were right yesterday," I told her. "I'm responsible for my own happiness, and being self-sufficient is the first step. It's time I picked up the pieces and got on with my life, but I can't do it without your help."

I paused and then continued. "You know, I would like to have a face again. I don't feel like I have an identity. I would give just about anything to be normal again."

Lauren was putting dishes in the dishwasher, and I was clumsily trying to help. We were both quiet for a minute, thinking about the difficult struggle that lay before me on my road to independence.

"You're right," she finally answered. "I don't want to hold you back. I'll give you all the support I can, but I wish you would wait a while before going out on your own."

As I had done so many times before, I found myself marveling at Lauren's kind heart. Her home had been a fortress to me. She and Anthony had protected me, dried my tears, fed me, clothed me, and loved me. I shuddered to think about where I would be if it weren't for the Jacobys. Now Lauren, with her tender heart, was afraid to let me go. But slowly and carefully, from that time on, she tried to prepare me for my readmittance into the real world.

EIGHT

"Surely there's a mask or something you could wear to cover your scars," Lauren called from the laundry room. It was the weekend, and she'd been busy all day washing clothes.

"The hospital says no," I replied, discouraged. "They said the only masks they have are for treatment right after an injury."

"Do you think we could make one?" Lauren asked.

"I don't know," I answered.

Lauren returned to the kitchen and set a laundry basket of clothes on the table. "I'm a good seamstress," she said. "I could make you one."

"It would mean a lot to me," I admitted. "I remember seeing other patients wearing masks at the burn center. I don't know where they got them, but they weren't the ones the hospital used for treatment."

"Do you remember what they looked like so you could show me?" she asked.

"They weren't very attractive, but at least the people who wore them didn't look like monsters," I replied. "Yes, I think I could show you what they looked like."

"Lauren?" Anthony called from the garage. The door to the kitchen was open, and he had been listening to our conversation while putting the lawn mower away. "Can I talk to you a minute?"

"Sure," Lauren said, entering the garage. "What's up?"

Anthony motioned for her to close the door, but I could still hear them talking even after the door was shut.

"I'm a little concerned about this mask business," he told her. "Jane can't go around wearing a mask for the rest of her life."

"What do you mean?" Lauren questioned.

"I mean that I don't think she needs to hide behind a mask—" he started to say.

"Do you know how hard it is for her to go into public looking like she does?" Lauren interrupted.

"No, but I can imagine," Anthony replied.

"Are you saying that she shouldn't let it bother her?" she asked, incredulous.

"Of course it's going to bother her," Anthony

responded. "It would bother anyone. What I'm saying is that she doesn't need to be ashamed of her scars—"

"Do you want her to stop wearing her wig, too?" Lauren interrupted crossly.

"Come on, Lauren!" Anthony pleaded. "Now you're being ridiculous! What about her wearing a little makeup? You can help her with that. Just keep it tasteful—"

"Yeah, sure!" Lauren replied sarcastically. "As if that will make everything right!"

"Let me ask you something," Anthony shot back. "Do you see the scars anymore? Well, I don't! I don't even notice them. And why don't I notice them? It's because I know Jane, and I love her for what she is, including her appearance. People— good, decent people—will accept her and love her for what she is."

Exasperated, Lauren said, "You don't understand! You just don't understand! This is her life we're talking about!"

"Yes, it is!" Anthony replied sharply. "Think about it, Lauren! Just think about it!"

"But—" Lauren began.

"No, this conversation is over," he told her. "Just think about what I've said."

I heard the screen door slam, and I knew

Anthony was outside again. Lauren came back into the kitchen. She looked defeated, but I could tell that Anthony's words were slowly making sense. She pulled out the kitchen chair next to me and sat down.

"I guess you heard us talking," she said, embarrassed. "These walls are paper thin, so you couldn't help but hear." Lauren sighed. "This is your choice, Jane," she continued, "not mine or Anthony's. If you want me to make you a mask, I will."

I nodded. I understood Anthony's reasoning, but I wasn't sure I had the courage to go into public looking like a freak.

"I want you to be happy, and I'll do anything I can to help you," Lauren added. She stood up, leaned over, and put her arms around me. I couldn't stop the tears from coming, so I put my arms around her and cried for the second time since the accident.

NINE

It took every ounce of courage I had, but I finally
came to terms with my appearance and ventured
forth into public—without a mask. That didn't mean
I no longer felt self-conscious about how I looked. It
just meant that I made a special effort to tolerate the
whispers and the stares and accept myself for what
I was.

I took driving lessons and got my driver's
license. I was tested to see what grade level in school
I was equal to, and I did surprisingly well. Under
the circumstances, the authorities saw no reason
not to give me a high school diploma. However,
my biggest problem wasn't in getting a diploma. I
quickly learned that no one took me seriously when
considering me for a job. I almost talked myself
into believing that no one would hire me because
they thought I would scare away their customers.
This, I hoped, was not true, but it didn't help my

self-esteem any. I was sick of people pointing and staring at me and tired of all the nasty remarks. I was so discouraged when I got home in the evenings that I was about ready to give up.

One evening, out of curiosity, I asked Lauren, "Did Kellie go to college?"

"Yes," she answered as we busily prepared dinner. "As a matter of fact, she majored in music. Dad called her his little nightingale because she had the voice of an angel. When she sang, it seemed as if the whole world stopped to listen. She would sing with so much feeling that it would take your breath away."

"Did you go to school?" I asked.

"Yes, I did," Lauren answered. "I majored in home economics. A lot of good that did me," she said, laughing.

We heard the garage door open and close, and we knew Anthony was home. Lauren had called him at his office and told him how discouraged I was.

"Hi, girls!" he said cheerfully as he entered the kitchen. He put his arms around Lauren and gave her a hug. "I told the kids to come in and wash up for supper," he added. He washed his hands, put on an apron, and started cutting tomatoes for the salad.

"I've been thinking, ladies," he said, "and I hate

to say this, but I'm afraid we're going to have to consider permanent disability for Jane."

Lauren was silent. "You know Jane doesn't want that," she finally remarked.

"I just don't know how she's going to get a job," he replied. "I know it sounds unfair, but it seems as if no one wants to give her a chance."

"What about school?" I asked. "Isn't there some way I could go to college?"

"That's an idea," Anthony said thoughtfully. "I don't know why I didn't think of that. Maybe I can look into it for you."

"How much does it cost to go to school nowadays?" Lauren questioned.

"I don't know, but I can find out," Anthony answered.

"What would you major in, Jane?" Lauren asked.

"Well," I replied, "I guess I could major in general education for now, and maybe I'll know exactly what I want later."

"That really isn't a bad idea," Anthony commented again. "Even a trade school would do for now. I'll make some calls tomorrow."

I was so excited at the prospect of going to school that I couldn't sleep that night. When I finally did get to sleep, I dreamed about forgotten locker combinations, attending school in my nightgown and slippers, and not being able to find my classes. I had good reason to be excited, because within the next couple of days, Anthony found a local university that would consider me for correspondence courses. If they accepted me, I could attend college from home. The best news was that the Mitchells agreed to pay for my first semester, with the understanding that my grades would be good enough to earn scholarships and grants for the rest of my schooling. I could hardly wait to get started. Things were finally looking up for me.

TEN

The following weeks were filled with apprehension as I nervously waited to receive word from the university. Lauren had insisted on inserting a note with my application to alert the staff and faculty of my situation (and as I found out later, she also called several of the school's administrators to inform them of my disabilities). She wanted my experience in college to be a good one, and she was willing to do everything in her power to make it as easy as possible for me.

Finally the letter of acceptance came, and I'd never seen a family so excited. Lacie and Matthew decorated a big banner with "Congratulations, Aunt Jane!" written on it, and Lauren prepared a feast for the evening meal, complete with cake and ice cream to celebrate.

"We knew you could do it, Aunt Jane!" Lacie exclaimed at the dinner table.

"Oh, well, let's not get our hopes up!" I said excitedly. "I haven't even begun the fight yet."

"But we're over the first obstacle," Lauren commented. Turning to her husband, she asked, "Isn't that right, Anthony?"

"I guess that's true," he answered. "My biggest concern was that the university wouldn't accept you because you didn't have records of any prior education. I think our worst fears are over. It's up to you now, Jane."

Because of my unique circumstances, I was required to meet with an on-campus counselor who would determine which classes were right for me and guide me through the registration process. I thought the day would never come. Night after night I tossed and turned in my bed, with nightmares robbing me of every fragment of my precious sleep. I couldn't remember a time when I had felt more excited, or more frightened. Finally the day arrived. Lauren wanted to come with me, but I made her promise that she would let me take the minivan and go alone. "I need the experience," I told her. "After all, I can't take you with me everywhere I go."

It was a crisp autumn morning, and I felt as if I'd been given a second chance at life. I buckled myself snugly into the seat belt, and with Lauren making a fuss over me about how nice I looked, I felt good about the day ahead. Just before I started the engine, she handed me her cell phone through the open window.

"Now don't forget to call me at noon if you aren't going to be home by then," she said. "And call me in the evening if you still aren't through. You know I'll worry."

"I will," I said, laughing nervously. "I'm going to be all right, honestly I am."

"Well, just the same, I still worry."

"Bye, Aunt Jane," Lacie called as she and Matthew ran up to the car. "We love you!"

"We love you," Matthew echoed his sister.

"I love you too," I answered, pleased with their concern. "And don't worry—I'll be home in time for dinner."

⁘ ⋄ ··· ⋄ ⁘

Once on campus, I got a lot of shocked stares. People were not accustomed to seeing someone like me wandering around the university. Most of them were compassionate and understanding, while others, in an attempt to be amusing, made nasty remarks that really hurt.

The meeting with my counselor, Aubree Roylance, went well. She spent several hours with me, taking me on a tour of the campus and introducing me to most of my professors. We had lunch together in one of the on-campus cafeterias. That's when I learned that Aubree was wearing a prosthetic leg. She carried herself so well that I never would have known if she hadn't told me.

Time passed quickly, and I suddenly realized that it was late afternoon. It had been a pleasant but tiring day, and I was glad it was over. Aubree walked with me to the administration building where we first met. She gave me a hug and told me she'd be in touch. Aubree was one of the most beautiful people I had ever known. I hoped to someday be as graceful and confident as she was, despite my deformities.

I could see the sun setting in the west as I looked out the big windows of the administration building. It was a beautiful sight. I scanned the boundless parking lot and realized that I had forgotten where I left the minivan.

"Leave it to me to do a stupid thing like this," I muttered. I would have to walk through the entire parking lot to find the car. I reached into my pocket for the gloves Lauren had put there in case I was late getting home and needed the warmth. As I pulled them out, I noticed that something else was in my pocket. It was then that I found what appeared to be the remains of a third glove. It was large and tan, soiled and worn. I couldn't figure out where it had come from. A devastating feeling came over me as I held it in my hand. It was almost as if at the very moment I touched its soft, worn material, I was racked with unbearable sorrow.

It's my imagination again, I thought, *probably one of Anthony's gloves that was put in my pocket by mistake.*

I caught my breath and quickly put the glove back where I'd found it. I pushed my way through the heavy glass doors, out into the crisp evening air.

I hadn't been outside for long when Lauren's cell phone rang. I clumsily answered it.

"Where are you?" Lauren asked from Anthony's cell phone.

"Oh, I've lost the car in this huge parking lot," I complained.

"Hold on," she replied. "I'll be right there!"

"You don't have to—" I tried to tell her.

"I don't have to come, but I want to," she hastily replied before hanging up.

In less than twenty minutes, Anthony, Lauren,

and the children pulled up alongside me in Anthony's company car.

"Boy, am I glad to see you!" I exclaimed.

"We were worried!" Lauren called through the open window.

"Can you help me find the car?" I asked, embarrassed. I was humiliated because I still hadn't found it.

Anthony laughed. "Hop in!" he said. "We'll find it in no time. You can tell us about your adventures while we're looking for it."

I rehearsed the entire day to them, down to the last detail—except for the part when I found the glove. The feeling I had when I pulled it out of my pocket frightened me, and I wanted to think about it before I discussed it with anyone. We quickly found the minivan but decided to come back for it.

"Where are we going, Daddy?" Lacie asked, noticing that we hadn't stopped for the car.

"We're going out to dinner," Anthony replied, "because Aunt Jane has had a rough day."

"All right!" Lacie said, sitting next to me in the back seat.

"All right!" echoed her little brother, who had recently taken up the habit of repeating everything he heard.

ELEVEN

I loved college. It seemed I couldn't learn fast enough. My first semester was coming to an end, and I was surprised to hear that my grade point average was 3.8. Paying for my next semester would be a breeze, because, thanks to Anthony helping me fill out the paperwork, I had already been awarded a scholarship and a grant.

Excitement was in the air, not just because of my success in school, but also because Christmas was on its way. I remembered how I had felt a year ago, and words could not express my gratitude to the Jacoby family for all they had done for me. Unfortunately, a part of me still longed to know who I was, and I spent many tearful hours grieving over what I had lost. It was on one such difficult night that I was finally willing to talk about the glove I found in my pocket. Anthony was out of town on business, so the timing couldn't have been better.

"Lauren?" I called softly as I knocked on her door.

"Come in," she answered. "It's open." Her light was on and she was reading. I sat down next to her on the bed.

"I hope I'm not disturbing you," I said quietly. "It's just that I really need to talk to someone."

"It's not a problem," she responded kindly. She looked at me as if she already knew what I was going to say, and I got right to the point.

"Where did the tan glove come from that I found in my pocket the day I went to register for school?" I asked.

She was quiet a minute, thinking about what she was going to say.

"When I picked you up at the hospital," she finally answered, "your therapist gave me the glove. She gave it to me along with the instructions to keep it until I thought you were ready for it."

Lauren paused. "Jane," she said, "it was clenched tightly in your fist when they pulled you out of the water. Since it appeared that you were already wearing gloves, they knew it belonged to someone else— possibly a loved one. No matter how hard they tried to pry it from your grasp, you wouldn't let go of it." Her gaze was fixed on me. "Do you remember whose glove it was?"

I hesitated before answering. "Something . . . strange happened when I pulled it out of my pocket," I said, pausing to collect my thoughts.

"Go on," she said gently.

"Such sadness . . ." I began. "I've never felt so devastated . . ." I paused again, trying to remember.

"Jane—?" Lauren questioned.

"I thought I remembered something when I first saw the glove, but I couldn't—"

"Was it something to do with a person?" she asked.

"I don't know," I replied.

"It's a man's glove. You must've been traveling with a man—"

"I just don't know," I said, shaking my head in frustration. "Sometimes I think I'm much better off not remembering."

"Well," Lauren said quietly, "why don't we talk about something else?" She looked at me and commented, "I'm really proud of you, sis."

For a moment, her words sounded so familiar that I was almost certain I'd heard them before. I caught my breath and squirmed uneasily.

"Is everything okay?" Lauren asked.

"What?" I responded, unsettled.

"I hope I haven't said something to upset you—" she started to say.

"No," I replied, quickly coming to my senses. "You were going to tell me what Santa is bringing the kids," I said, clumsily changing the subject.

Lauren smiled. "Yes, I'll tell you what Santa is bringing the kids, but first you have to let me read to you. I'm reading *Jane Eyre*." She pulled the covers down, patted the bed next to her, and motioned for me to join her. I accepted the invitation and climbed in.

"I know it was hard for you to talk to me tonight," she said once we were comfortable, "but I believe that the day will come when you will remember your past, and it will bring you comfort and peace instead of heartache." With that said, Lauren opened the book and read:

"I am coming!" I cried. "Wait for me! Oh, I will come;" I flew to the door, and looked into the passage: it was dark. I ran out into the garden: it was void.

"Where are you?" I exclaimed.

The hills beyond Marsh Glen sent the answer faintly back—"Where are you?" I listened. The wind sighed low in the firs; all was moorland loneliness and midnight bush."

TWELVE

In the early hours of the morning, my bedroom door opened, and Lacie quietly entered the room. I didn't realize I was crying in my sleep, but Lacie had heard me and was concerned.

"Aunt Jane," she said, her voice trembling. "It makes me so sad to hear you cry at night. What's the matter? You can tell me. I won't tell."

I sat up in bed and drew her close to me. "Oh, Lacie!" I exclaimed. "You're such a sweetheart! I wish I could explain."

"I think I know why," she answered, and bringing her dimpled hand out from behind her, she held an object out to me. "Here," she said, placing it in my hand. "It's yours. I think I'm old enough now that I don't need it."

"What's this?" I asked, trying to see it in the dark.

"It's a nightlight," she answered. "Aunt Kellie gave it to me before she left to go to school."

"What a thoughtful gesture," I said. "Are you sure you want me to have it?"

"You can have it," she assured me. "You're afraid of the dark, aren't you? It's awful dark in here, and I would cry and be afraid too, if Mama and Daddy weren't in the room next to me. Here, I'll plug it in for you." She took the light and groped her way through the darkness to the electrical outlet. "There," she said, turning it on. "Now you won't be afraid anymore."

"Thank you, Lacie!" I exclaimed and gave her a hug. "I'm so lucky to have you! I love you so much!"

"I'll stay with you tonight," she said quietly. "Remember the time you stayed with me when I was feeling bad? Well, I'll do the same for you."

"Okay," I replied, pulling the covers back and helping her climb into the bed. "It will be nice to have some company!"

"What should we talk about?" she asked.

"Oh, I don't know," I answered. "Why don't you tell me about school?"

"All right," she replied sleepily. But Lacie's little whispers were audible only momentarily, for she was soon fast asleep on my shoulder.

❧ ◇ • • • ◇ ❧

I awoke a few hours later and realized that my arm had gone to sleep. I carefully tried to move it without waking Lacie, and in so doing, my eye caught sight of the nightlight. I gasped softly as a feeling of déjà vu hit me again. Something about the light shining in the darkness was familiar to me. *But why?* I wondered. I stared at it for several seconds, but the feeling went away as quickly as it had come. For the rest of the night I was left to ponder what a glove and a nightlight had to do with my past.

THIRTEEN

I hated to see such a beautiful day come to an end. It was three days before Christmas, and Lauren and Anthony and I were returning home from a Christmas concert at the university. For the first time in two years, I was excited about my future, and I could hardly wait for Christmas morning so I could see the children's faces when they opened their gifts from Santa.

Lauren and Anthony were singing Christmas carols, and I tried to join in every so often. We were almost home when we noticed smoke coming from what appeared to be our neighborhood.

"What do you suppose it is?" Lauren asked, concerned.

"I don't know," Anthony replied, and the minivan picked up speed. A tense silence filled the car as we quickly made our way toward home.

"It's our house!" Lauren exclaimed as we turned

the corner and the source of the smoke came into view.

The fire engine had not arrived, but the entire neighborhood was standing in front of the Jacoby residence watching the flames leap from what had once been the family room. Lauren, Anthony, and I desperately searched for two children and their babysitter. We found Lacie and Maria, but no Matthew.

"Oh, Mrs. Jacoby," Maria cried hysterically. "The children put the candles in the window and the curtains caught fire. I told them several times not to put them there, but they did it anyway!"

"Why were the candles lit?" Anthony exclaimed, but Maria was too hysterical to answer.

"Where's our Matthew?" Lauren said over and over again, but no one seemed to be listening.

"He's in the house!" Lacie said, crying. "He put the fire in the window, Mama, so he went back in to put it out so he wouldn't get in trouble."

"No! No! Not my baby!" Lauren cried, and she pushed her way through the crowd toward the door.

"Lauren!" Anthony exclaimed, catching her arm and holding her back. "I'll go! You stay here!"

I didn't hesitate. As far as I was concerned, Matthew was not going through what I had been through. Before anyone could stop me, I stumbled across the lawn and through the front door. Something—or someone—told me to drop to my knees, and so I did. By instinct, I started to pray, harder than I'd ever prayed before. I crawled toward the family room where I thought Matthew might be.

The smoke was so heavy that I didn't know if either one of us would survive. It was difficult for me to see, and I was having trouble breathing.

As it grew hotter around me, I became another person, at another time, and I suddenly remembered being strapped into the seat of an airplane. I was holding someone's hand, and on that hand was a tan glove. It was unbearably hot, and my companion and I knew that the plane was in flames and on its way into the river.

As my memory became more vivid, the heat from the fire intensified. I remembered a sudden, violent impact, and the freezing water gradually covering my body until I was totally immersed in the river. I struggled with my seat belt, never once letting go of the hand that wore the tan glove. After freeing myself, I immediately tried to free my companion, but it was no use. To my horror, I realized that the person whose life I was desperately trying to save was already dead. In one split second I made my decision. I would stay there, underwater, and die with him.

It was dark inside the wreckage, but everything around me was suddenly illuminated. I looked up and saw a light shining down through the water. It grew brighter and brighter until I was completely engulfed in it. Someone grabbed the back of my coat and pulled me from the debris. Within seconds I broke surface. The man who freed me quickly lifted me into the waiting arms of a paramedic hanging from a helicopter. I never saw my deliverer again.

I was torn from the horrible memory of my past by the sound of a child crying. There, curled up on the floor, was Matthew. I crawled toward him. I had not taken thought as to how I would get him out of the house. I didn't have much strength, and I was in a great deal of pain already because of my previous injuries. I knew it wasn't going to be easy to get both of us out alive. We were both coughing, and it was almost impossible to breathe. I quickly contemplated my alternatives, and finally, with the guidance of that same influence that had directed me to drop to the floor when I first entered the house, I helped him climb on my back.

Crawling on my hands and knees, I painfully carried him out of the room and down the hall. It was then that I realized we weren't going to make it.

"Please, God!" I cried between coughs. "Please let Matthew live. He's just a little boy. . . ."

"Don't cry, Aunt Jane," Matthew said softly. I could feel his little face next to mine. He let go of my neck and patted my cheek reassuringly. "Everything is going to be all right," he promised. "I think Jesus is here." His hand slowly fell limp at my side, and I knew he'd lost consciousness. *I have failed*, I thought, my heart breaking. *Lauren and Anthony will lose their precious son, and I can't do anything about it.*

"Why, God?" I whispered. "Why?"

With all hope of survival diminished, I slowly lowered my body onto the floor. The smoke enveloped us, and I felt light-headed and nauseated.

What happened next was nothing short of a miracle. Half asleep, half awake, I felt someone lift Matthew off my back. Someone else picked me up and carried me toward the garage. I didn't know who was helping us. All I knew was that we were safe, and we were going to be all right.

Then I passed out.

FOURTEEN

I dreamed I was home again, a teenager, in my bedroom, on my bed. The door opened and a man stood silhouetted in the light.

"Sweetheart," he said gently. "Don't cry. There will be other proms and other young men. You mustn't take this so hard."

"Daddy," I cried, but like all dreamers, the words were trapped in my throat and I couldn't utter a sound.

He came to me and sat down on the edge of my bed. I felt his warm hand on my forehead and could see his face clearly. Though my dream had erased the years from his features, I still recognized his well-beloved face.

It was once again the night of my junior prom, and a boy I had a crush on had just broken our date for the dance. My grief was my father's grief, and in his own loving way he was endeavoring to ease my pain and disappointment.

"Listen," he said, "do you hear the sound of a bird singing?"

No words would escape my lips, and, try as I might, I couldn't lift my arms to embrace him.

"It's the song of a nightingale," he continued. "And do you feel the darkness?" he asked. "I've never felt a darker night."

I strained to hear the song of the bird, and faintly, through the moonless night, I heard its beautiful cadence. It was soft and sad, melodious and clear, pure and true. Though the darkness had enveloped me, I was not afraid, for a light was emanating from the face of my father who held me in his arms as he sat next to me on the bed.

"The nightingale sings his most beautiful song when the night is darkest," he said softly. "You and I have just witnessed one of God's greatest symphonies. I want you to be like that nightingale. When things get their blackest, don't stop singing—just sing from your heart. God will hear your song and answer it with a blessing on your head."

The song of the bird was slowly fading, and so was the image before me. But as it faded, I heard my father, Mr. Mitchell, say, "Just like the lonely nightingale, we each need to experience darkness to appreciate light."

"Daddy," I called from lips that had no sound. "Daddy, help me, I'm lost!" I reached out to him, but he was gone.

$$\sim \diamond \cdots \diamond \sim$$

I suddenly awoke. It was dark, and it took me a few seconds to realize where I was. I could hear someone singing Christmas carols, and for a moment, I believed I had dreamed the entire last year of my life.

The hospital? I thought, panicking. *Not again! I can't go through this again!*

I painfully remembered all that had transpired on the day of the crash. Michael, my fiancé, had been at my side in that ill-fated plane. After getting engaged a few days before Christmas, we decided to surprise both our families with a visit. Mike had already booked his flight, and when someone canceled their reservation at the last minute, he persuaded me to take it. We would visit his family and make our announcement, and then we would continue on home to my family and give them the good news. My seat wasn't next to his, but a kind elderly woman graciously offered to trade so I could sit next to him on our flight. It was an oversight on the part of the airlines, for they had somehow failed to record my name in their flight manifest. One seat was listed as being empty, and it was the seat I had traded to the elderly woman. Her remains, along with all other victims and survivors, had been identified, but no one knew who I was, where I had come from, or where I was going.

Recollections of my past came flooding back, as if a dam had burst and its waters could no longer be restrained. I tried to control the despair that consumed me, but it was no use. My heart raced and my head throbbed. I was so sick! I could hear Lauren calling my name, but I couldn't see her. I felt her hand on mine, but in my delirium I thought I was imagining it. In shock, my body shook uncontrollably, and the warning device on the medical equipment near my bed sounded its alarm. Within seconds, hospital personnel surrounded me. I tried to call out, but no sound came. I felt hopeless and utterly alone. Quickly losing consciousness, I gave in to the darkness.

FIFTEEN

My spirit was at peace. I was weightless and felt no pain. I looked down at my body and saw the doctors and nurses desperately trying to save my life—a life I didn't feel was worth saving. I saw Lauren, pushed aside, and standing in the corner. She was crying. Oh, how I wanted to hold and comfort her! I wanted to tell her I was okay and no longer felt pain.

I noticed Lacie's glowing nightlight that she must have brought to the hospital for my benefit—a reminder that I had never really been alone. I vividly recalled giving it to her one night when she was afraid of the dark.

I saw the Christmas tree in the lounge and heard carolers singing "Silent Night."

Santa was in the children's ward, holding the children on his lap, asking them what they wanted for Christmas and handing out candy.

I could hear and see Lacie and Anthony in Matthew's hospital room. I was relieved to know that he wasn't burned, but I somehow knew that his lungs would need time to heal. Unaware of what was happening in the ICU, the three of them were laughing at the cartoons they were watching on the TV hanging from the wall. I wanted to say good-bye and tell them I loved them, but something was pulling me away.

A soft, familiar voice called my name. It was indistinct at first but then grew clearer. A light appeared above me, and I was quickly drawn toward it. I suddenly found myself standing before the most beautiful being I had ever seen. He was glorious beyond description. Though I stood at more than an arm's length from him, I could feel his warm embrace and his overpowering love.

"Lord—" I said, reaching out to him.

"Kellie, do you love me?" he asked tenderly.

"You know I love you," I answered.

"Then feed my sheep."

His reply was simple, yet I did not understand.

"I want to come home," I said, not wanting to leave him. "Please don't send me away. There is so much pain!"

"You must not be afraid to live. Twice I spared your life in the flames, and this I did for a purpose.

There are still many things for you to learn and do."

He smiled at me, and I felt an indescribable peace.

"Do you love me, Kellie?" He asked again.

"Yes, Lord. You know I love you!"

"Then feed my sheep," he repeated. "Understand, Kellie, that one of the greatest gifts I have given my children is the gift of each other."

He took me in his arms and embraced me, and then I felt myself quickly being drawn from his presence. As his light faded into the night, I distinctly heard the words, "I will always be there for you . . ."

SIXTEEN

Idon't know how long I was unconscious, but it seemed only minutes before I woke up. Lauren was sitting next to me, holding my hand. My mother was sitting on the other side of the bed, holding my other hand, and my father, Anthony, and the children were also there.

"I told you it was Aunt Kellie. I knew it was her," Lacie said tearfully.

"Lauren," I whispered weakly. "Lauren."

"Kellie," she cried, weeping for joy. "You're awake!" Turning to Anthony, she excitedly said, "She's awake! Go get the doctor!" Anthony immediately headed for the nurses' station. Everyone started talking at once and calling my name. My parents were crying and reaching for me. They all took their turn at holding and touching me. I'd never felt so loved in my life.

Quickly coming to my senses, I looked up at my

sister and faintly asked, "How did you know?"

"Lacie told us you were crying and talking in your sleep the other night. You kept repeating the name Mike. I wish she would've told us sooner, but she didn't think it was important. Kellie was seriously dating a Michael, and we were expecting a marriage proposal any day." Then she added, "In my heart I knew you were Kellie the minute I saw you sitting in that chair with your face to the wall. I was so afraid I was wrong and it was my imagination. God heard and answered our prayers, and we were led to you."

"Mom," I said, with tears streaming down the sides of my face, "Michael is dead."

"I know," she replied, her voice breaking, "and I'm so sorry."

"He asked me to marry him, and we were flying home for Christmas to surprise everyone. I should've let you know, but I never dreamed—"

"It's all right," she answered, tenderly taking me in her arms. "Everything is going to be all right. You're home now, Kellie." And with my family standing nearby, my mother gently rocked me in her arms to the cadence of a nightingale's song drifting on the breeze through an open window.

EPILOGUE

The years have come and gone since my tragedy. My face and most of my body have been reconstructed through plastic surgery. I have accepted the fact that things will never be the same, but I also know without a doubt that people can be happy regardless of their circumstances.

Since that night so long ago, I've graduated from college with a master's degree in social work. I can honestly say that I have done everything in my power to feed the Lord's sheep.

No one knows who carried Matthew and me out of Lauren's burning house to safety. Many of our acquaintances refuse to believe that a supreme being intervened. The firefighters found us in the backyard and assumed that I had done it, but that's not what happened. I would be lying, not only to myself, but also to God, if I said otherwise.

I have been to Michael's grave and have

considered visiting his parents, but I always dismiss the idea for fear of opening old wounds. It was not the right time for Michael and me, but I am confident that our time will come.

As for my sister, Lauren, I owe her and her little family much more than I will ever be able to repay. If it wasn't for their undying love, faith, and prayers, I would not be here today to tell my story. Her Christlike example of love and compassion have taught me the true meaning of the word charity. One small act of kindness can greatly influence the life of another human being. We must do all we can to help our fellow man.

We have often discussed the miracle of the nightingale singing outside my hospital room on Christmas Eve. How a window was open on a cold night in December is a mystery to us. Even more baffling is that to our knowledge there is no such bird found there, and to this day we have no explanation for its mysterious presence. The message of the bird's song rings clear and true to me even now. Yes, little nightingale, I too will sing again someday!

I have learned many things through my experience—things I will never forget, including the reality that bad things sometimes happen to good people. Life does not end with the grave, and nothing escapes the eyes of God—not even a fallen sparrow. But most of all, I will always remember my glimpse into heaven, when I learned the simple truth that one of God's greatest gifts to us, his children, is the gift of each other.

ABOUT THE AUTHOR

Heather is the fifth of seven children born to John and Raeola Holm. She attended grade school in Springville, Utah, and studied music at Brigham Young University. In her younger years, she played the guitar and wrote and performed her own music.

While attending Brigham Young University, Heather worked for *The Springville Herald* and became interested in editing and writing. She still enjoys music, but the printing and publishing business has provided a good living for her for the past thirty-six years.

Heather is currently serving as the managing editor of a publishing company in Utah County. She is the author of *Against an Amber Sky*, *Discovering the Magic of Christmas*, and *Forever Santa*.

PM 22
May og
Sat

62
11390483
9505513188932

0 26575 59124 8